Unsaid truth

Kayla Colson

Contents

Chapter One

Part~1

"Uff mom dad it's totally fine. I can manage don't worry too much ok" Ayesha said to her parents. As she is going to Italy.

Introduction-

Ayesha Bora, a 22 years Indian girl , she done her btech from one of the well respective college in india. She is good at studies that's why she got opportunity to work in Italy.

Her parents don't want her to go Italy but she is stubborn. And One of the main reason to go Italy is finding her dream Mafia Man.

Yes Ayushi live in her dream Land or you can say delulu world. She is a reader and expect those frictional things to happen in real life And parents are aware of their daughter very well that's the reason they don't want her to leave alone in a unknown country but after getting a biggest opportunity her parents somewhere agree.

In airport-

"Now don't worry ok, i will come back soon" Ayesha hug her parents before leaving.

Time skipped to Italy-

Ayesha Pov- Uff finally I'm in italy. Now i can find my perfect hot cold fictional Mafia man.

I already had some Italian friends so they come to pick me and it didn't effect me much as they help me to find a place and help me to shift my stuffs.

"Lorenzo, Jessica thank you so much. You guys help me very much. I'm glad" Ayesha said to her friends.

Jessica- ok ok but you have to give us a welcome party

Ayesha- i think you guys should give me a welcome party as i come in italy right

Lorenzo- Damn girl ayesha is right tho.

Jessica- Ok than tomorrow you will go to club

Ayesha- guys i have to join my office tomorrow i don't think. I can manage time.

Jessica- than next weekend

Ayesha- great

Lorenzo- Ok i will bring some of my friends too

Ayesha- Bring me a mafia also

Lorenzo- You want to die girl

Ayesha- No bring a good mafia

Jessica- ughhh this girl. Lorenzo let's go let her live in her dreamland.

Jessica and lorenzo went to their place. As ayesha check her whole belongings and went to sleep.

Next morning~

Ayesha pov- i couldn't sleep properly last night because many things were coming inside my mind. At 1st i was excited but now I'm Missing my parents and also little bit scared. Cause i don't know anyone rather than jessica and Lorenzo. But i have to manage now. This is my new life style.

I wake up get fresh and straightly went to my new company. I was little nervous because everyone is talking in Italian language and i can't speak Italy.

At office i made some new friends as they are really nice, they talk to me really nicely and i got comfortable with them. They teach me my work and other employee were also good

Time skipped to weekend~

On call-

Jessica- what the hell girl, where were you ?

Ayesha- i was about to call you but

Jessica- but what ? You were busy with your new friends i know

Ayesha- it's not like that , i was busy because they were teaching me about my work and all

Jessica- ok ok no need to explain and be ready at 8 pm. Lorenzo will come to pick you

Ayesha- what

Jessica- you forgot ? Your welcome party

Ayesha- ooo yes yes i remember. And jessica please tell Lorenzo to bring me a mafia ok ?

Jessica - silly girl

She cut the call. They know how much ayesha love mafia and wanted to meet a real life mafia. But everything is not how she reads on book. The dark and crual side is very different than she thought.

I got ready i wear a long black dress and a little bit of makeup. I never wear makeup so much as my skin is very sensitive.

I got a call from Lorenzo. He is waiting for me outside.

Lorenzo- Damn girl you're looking hot

Ayesha- I'm Born to be hot

Lorenzo- Ahhm this girl. Let's go jessica is waiting for us

Ayesha- Yup let's go

Lorenzo and i went inside the club. This is giving me full party vibes, everyone is dancing drinking. They are having their fun time. As i walk in i saw jessica sitting with some other people.

Jessica saw me and she walk towards me

Jessica- damn girl you're looking sexy

Ayesha- Not more than you *I winked at her making her laught*

Lorenzo- girls let's go i will introduce you to my friends

Lorenzo introduce me with some of his friends. They are also pretty good. We are dancing like crazy. The whole week i spent doing only office work and today i will just enjoy.

Jessica- bitch drink it

I take the glass from jessica hand and drink it

Ayesha- Damn it's good

I started drinking more , i couldn't control myself not to drink

Lorenzo- girl stop drinking. Let's go and play a game

Jessica- ye_s that's so_unds good

Jessica and i aren't in our senses

Lorenzo take us towards his friends

- let's play a game

Lorenzo- let's play truth and dare

- ok but only dare not truth

- that's sounds good

The bottle spin. 1st round jessica

Jessica- bitch why me first

Lorenzo- because it's your luck bitch

Jessica- ugghhhh my head is paining. Do it first

- drink this whole bottle

Ayesha- Noo it's too much don't drink baby

Jessica- babe don't worry. He will pay for this bottle. I will drink it anyway it's free

Everyone laught while jessica drink the whole bottle in 3min

Everyone is laughing enjoying doing their dares and the bottle spin and this time it stop towards me

Jessica- finally it's my bitch timeee

Lorenzo- haha you're laughing at me now i will give you a dare

Ayesha- keep it simple haa please

• Showing them my puppy eyes but they seems not to care*

Lorenzo- ok ayesha you have to go and sit in a stranger lap

Ayesha- what the hell

Jessica- yes it fun do it ayesha

Ayesha- are you guys want me to get beaten

Lorenzo- off course not

Jessica- don't worry no one will mind. Just sit for 10 sec and run from there ok

Ayesha- I will kill you guys

I have no other options as everyone is just having fun. And i don't wanna ruin the fun so i also angree

I went towards the dance floor and in the other side there is two man standing and one of them is sitting on the couch, i didn't think much and direct went towards him and sit on his lap. I can feel his heartbeat, he stop his motion and i can feel he is looking at my face before he could say anything i run from there as fast as i could i don't even look at him.

Jessica- ouhh girl you're on fire

Lorenzo- Dudeee just ugh i can't say anything. Did you notice how that man is looking at her

Jessica- haha it's fun tho

Ayesha- Stop it guys my heart is beating so fast

Jessica- yes yes let's go now it's getting late

With that me jessica and lorenzo went out from the club. They left me in my apartment

Next morning-

Ayesha Pov- Ugghh my head is so paining

I got a notification from my company they select me for a new project, i was jumping on my bed than I checked the time. Holy shit i only have 1 hours left. I run to the bathroom , get fresh and without having breakfast i run to my office.

Chapter Two

Part~2

I came inside the office and run towards my desk. I put my bag there and went towards the manager office.

Ayesha- Sir

Manager- Ayesha i was searching for you, come let's go Our CEO must reach by now

Me and manager is going towards the meeting rooom while the manager said.

Manager- You are lucky, to have this great opportunity

Ayesha- thank you sir

Manager- Our CEO never allow newly join employee to work in new project but this time they choose new employee.

He said to you making you confused because you thought maybe manager recommend your name for new project but he didn't. You thinking about that when the manager call you

Manager- let's go inside

Ayesha- yes sir

As i walk inside i can see there are more than 10 people sitting, i walk towards them and take a sit next to an employee. Everyone is seem to nervous and little bit of scared but i am excited. Yes I'm very excited as i have been always seen in movies an independent woman working for herself. I always want to have a life like that and now it's actually happening, i was in my fantasy but soon my thoughts got interrupt. I look at the entrance door and someone walk in. Everyone stood up from there place so did i. I was looking at him, he is tall, very tall, a perfectly build body, i can see his abs through his black coat, he has dark brown eyes and Dark black hair. I was mesmerized by his looked. I was Staring at him samelessly and soon our eyes meet making me divert my eyes.

He come and sit in front of us like a king. Now i understand why everyone is so nervous. His aura is dominating that made everyone scared of him. He didn't even ulter a word and everyone is shivering. I don't understand why so scared of this handsome man

- Good morning everyone*Cold as ice*

Everyone- Good morning Sir

Adriano- I'm adriano Romano, Your CEO. Some of you had already work with me and for some this is first time. I hope none of you would make any mistakes.

Everyone nodded

CEO Manager- "XYZ" This project is very important for our company. So don't make any mistakes. You all have to work individually. I will give each of you 5 files and complete those files within a week

Everyone nodded

Adriano- Anyone has any questions if yes you can ask me right now

Everyone is silent but

Ayesha- Sir

Everyone looking at her with wided eyes

Ayesha- mm actually it's my first time. If someone can help me in understanding the process than it will help me

Adriano- Don't worry. You can ask anyone. I'm sure everyone will help you

Ayesha noddes with a smile

Everyone is looking at her for her braveness. She didn't even hesitate before saying anything infront him.

After the meeting everyone start taking leave. As i was walk out from the meeting room a boy come towards me

- hi

Ayesha- hello

Sam- My name is sam. Nice to meet you

Ayesha- my name is ayesha

Sam- you're quite impressive

Ayesha- haha thank you

Sam- you're the first employee who dare to ask Mr Romano something

Ayesha- why ? Why so ? Mr Romano said that ask if you have anything that's why i ask. Did i made any mistakes

Ayesha said looking at sam eyes making sam chuckle

Sam- No that's not what i means by the way don't tell me you're new here and don't know anything about Mr Romano

Ayesha- unfortunately yes I'm new here

Sam- what *sam said with wided eyes*

Sam- this is first time a new employee is working with Mr Romano new project

Ayesha- i don't understand what you mean?

Sam- Mr Romano never appoint new employee for his project. He always choose experience employee or you can say who work in this company for more than 5 years. I work with Mr Romano for 2 time and it's very difficult. You know why everyone fear him because he don't hesitate to take there job away. If you made any mistakes he might fire you also

Ayesha- Shit why me ? Why they select me ? I'm not that impressive nor I'm talented ugghh i just come here 1 week ago i want to go home this soon.

Sam- No no don't think too much ok. Ask me if you need any help

Ayesha- thank you, i will

I went towards my desk and sit there. I'm hungry as i don't eat anything from morning but now i have to wait lunch time.

I was doing my work but our manager come towards my desk

Manager- Ayesha

Ayesha- yes sir

Manager- You have to move in 7 floor

Ayesha- but why sir

Manager- as your working for the new project with Mr Romano so you should have to move there.

Ayesha- ohh i understand sir

The guards help me to take my stuff. I sattle everything in my new desk. I was just looking around the place there is not too many people and everyone is busy in there work. I sit on my place and looked at my side and my eyes got widen. The CEO office room is in front of my desk. What the hell is happening ugghhh

Chapter Three

Part~3

I was working on some files than i got a call on my desh

Ayesha- Hello

- Come to my cabin

Cut the call

I got confused which cabin ? Who call me ? I call back again

Ayesha- which cabin sir ?

Adriano- I'm Adriano come to my cabin

Oooh shot why I'm so stupid ughh i grab my hair in frustration.

I should go now. I run to his office this is first time I'm going to face him Alone and i already made a stupid mistake. Please good don't take my job

I checked myself and knock on the door

Ayesha- May i come in sir ?

Adriano- come in !

Damn his voice is so cold

I Walk inside the cabin

Ayesha- Sorry sir i didn't know that you call me

Adriano- Hmm take these files and complete them within an hour

Ayesha- all of these

I widen my eyes because that's alot of files how can i manage to do it all in an hour

Adriano- yes

He is not even looking at me. This cold ass i thought he would be nice like all other people but nah i was wrong he is worst ughh , i curse him more than 100 time in my mind.

Ayesha- oh ok sir

I take the files and went out from his office

Ayesha- i think i have to stay hungry today. Why good why ughh.

I was doing my work as i only have an hour but someone put coffee on my table i look up to see the person and it's sam

Sam- Have it

Ayesha- thank you sooo much sam

Sam- look like someone give you alot of work

Ayesha- Yesss

I grab the coffee cup and smile at him.

Sam- tell me if you need any help

Ayesha- Okk

Sam went towards his desk and i also start working again.

Lunch break~

It's already lunch time and I'm still not done with my work yet. My hungry also i haven't eat anything yet.

I think i should go and eat something first and let's see what happen, at least i should eat something before dying.

I was about to go but i heard Mr Romano yelling at someone.

I sit back at my place

Ayesha- No no food is important but i don't wanna get scolded by Mr Romano.

I again started doing my work, everyone is leaving for lunch and here I'm doing this stupid work.

" You should go and have you lunch" i look up and show Mr Romano.

I stood up at my place.

Ayesha- ye_s sir i mean no sir.. aa i mean i have alot of work to cover sir. If i had...

Mr Romano didn't let me finish my word

Mr Romano- Go and have it

Saying that he went away from my desk. I'm happy that at least I'm gonna have my lunch.

He is not that bad tho.

I went to have my lunch.

After lunch~

Ughh I'm feeling sleepy i think i eat too much now. First i didn't have time to eat and now i eat too much. Why I'm like this.

Still i have to do my work. I was doing my work but again i got a call

Adriano- come to office now.

Before i can say anything Mr Romano cut the call. What am i gonna say to him ughh I'm not done yet. There are so many files left.

I don't have any other options rather than go to his office.

I knock on the door

Adriano- come in

Ayesha- Sir actually

Adriano- what ? *He looked at me making me shivering in fear*

I looked down

Adriano- Miss Ayesha you are not done with the work i give ?

Ayesha- No sir actually some files are left

Adriano- Hmm them before leaving office

Ayesha- Yes sir i will

I went out from Mr Romano office

Ugh I'm lucky today he didn't shout at me. But i have to complete this stupid files before going home or this time he will Surely eat me alive.

I was busy doing my work and didn't notice the time. Everyone started leaving from work and here I'm completing my last file.

Sam- Ayesha not done yet

Ayesha- Almost

Sam- Let me help you

Ayesha- thanks sam but this is last file I'm almost done just have to check once again

Sam- Ok if you say so

I smile at him

Sam- i should leave than see you tomorrow

Ayesha- Yup bye

Sam left office, now only I'm left in the whole floor But what if ghost attact me. No no i should complete this file and run to my house.

After some time later~

Finally I'm done.

I walk towards Mr Romano office and knock on the door

Adriano- come in

Ayesha- sir I'm done checking the files

I placed the files to his desk

Adriano nodded

Ayesha- sir may i leave now

Adriano- Yes go and booked a cab it's quite late

Ayesha- yes sir

I walk out from his office. Huhh that the hell me think about himself he fucking give me so much work , just because of him I'm late and now he cared.

Chapter Four

Part~4

The next morning~

Ayesha pov- today i wake up at time because i don't want to get scold by Mr angry. Yes i give him a nice name and it suits him very well

I get ready and went to office.

I was doing my work than a female employee come towards me and tell me that Mr Romano call me in his cabin.

Ayesha- May i come in sir

Adriano- come in

Ayesha- yes sir how may i help you

Adriano- bring me a cup of coffee

Ayesha- sorry

Adriano- i said bring me a cup of coffee

Ayesha-ooh ok

I didn't say anything further and quickly went from his cabin

Ayesha- What the hell he think about himself huhh do i look like his assistant. That he order me. He is such a jerk ughh i hate him so much.

In cafeteria~

Ayesha- one cup of coffee please

Employee- ma'am sugar

Ayesha- 3 tablespoons

Employee- ok ma'am

I don't know he like sugar or not out of blue i said 3 tablespoons. I take the cup and went inside his cabin

Ayesha- Sir your coffee

I put the cup in his desk

Adriano- You have done many mistakes Miss ayesha

Ayesha- sorry sir but what are you saying ?

I asked him being confused

Adriano- you have to do this files again

My eyes widen as i work so hard on these files.

I was thinking about the files than Mr angry drink the coffee and in within a second he looked at me like a lion. I gulped down my own saliva.

Adriano- what is this

Ayesha- si_r co_ffee

Adriano- i know but who told you to put sugar

Ayesha- No one

Adriano- than why did you put sugar

Ayesha- but sir you didn't even told me to not put

Adriano is looking at me with shock Eyes. It's seems like he want to say something but at the same time he also don't want to.

Adriano- leave it and take this files and this time don't make any mistakes

Ayesha- ok sir

I grab the files quickly and straightly went to my desk.

Sam- hello

Ayesha- hi

Sam- what are you doing

Ayesha- Mr angry told me to do this files again.

Sam- haha mr angry are you talking about mr Romano

Ayesha- yes he always stay angry so i give him a nick name

Sam laugh while looking at me

Ayesha- why are you laughing is not a joke

Sam- yes yes i understand

Ayesha- i work so hard on these files now i have to do this again.

Sam- let me help you

Ayesha- ok but what about your work

Sam- me don't worry about it. I can manage

Ayesha- ok if you say so.

Sam is helping me to do the files correctly. We are almost done with the files. I like how sam is helping me. He is really nice tho.

We were almost done with the files but i got flinch when i heard

Adriano- miss ayesha.

I look up and saw Mr angry looking at me angrily

Ayesha- Ye_s sir

Adriano- care to explain why Mr sam is helping you rather than doing his work

Ayesha- sir ac_tually

Sam- Sir actually i insists to help her. She was having difficulty so i decided to help

Adriano- if you have any problems why don't you ask me miss ayesha. I'm your boss right

Ayesha- I'm sorry sir

Adriano- sam you do your work and next time i don't have to tell the same thing again

Sam- ok sir

Adriano went inside his cabin and sam went towards his desk.

Ayesha pov- ughhh really he was just helping me. Look like i have to do all this myself.

Chapter Five

Part~5

In meeting room~

Adriano~ From today onwards we are going to work on our project and i hope no one gonna make any mistakes.

Everyone nodded.

After the meeting end i was going towards canteen to have my lunch but i got a call from mr angry and he order me to come inside his cabin

Ayesha- Yes sir

Adriano- miss ayesha can you please bring my lunch

Ayesha- sir it's not my job it's your secretary job

Adriano- i know and she is absent for some day so i decided to make you my Temporary secretary.

Ayesha- ooh ok sir i will bring you lunch

I bow at him and went out from his cabin

Ayesha pov- this jerk what the hell he think of himself does he think himself a king or what. How can he order me like that do i look like his maid uggghhhhhhhh

I walk inside the canteen and started putting food on the plate, i was done but then my eyes shifted towards the spicy section. I walk towards that and grab some red chili peppers and started pouring on the soup. I was 100% confident with my work.

Haha now you will never let me do your stupid work.

After knocking i went inside his cabin and put the food on his desk and give him a sweet smile.

Ayesha- enjoy your food sir

Adriano nodded and i walk out from there

I was sitting on the desk and continuously looking the his cabin door waiting for him to run out from there but suddenly my phone ring.

Ayesha- hello

Adriano- come to my cabin now

Today he will fire me

I walk inside his cabin and he is looking at me like he will eat me in next second

I grader all my courage and asked

Ayesha- sir

Adriano- Shut up

* He shout at me for the first time. Now i can feel i messed up very badly*

Adriano- why did you do that lunch

Ayesha- i don't know sir

Adriano- are you kidding me

Ayesha- no sir yes sir. Please sir sorry sir i will not do that sir forgive me sir

I was saying whatever coming to my mouth without realizing

Adriano- this is your Last warning

Ayesha nodded being all scared

Adriano- you can go now

I run from there. I was so stupid how can i do that to my own boss ooh god my mind was on vacation that's why i make this kind of mistakes but he forgive me and give me one last warning, now i will not make any mistakes i don't want to get fire

I was sad for rest of the day i don't know why i feel sad when he shout at me but i have to make sure i don't make this kind of mistake again.

The next day~

I was sad because what happen yesterday but i have to focus on my work because it's new project and i don't want to get scold by him.

I was focusing on my work and i didn't even notice the time but soon i got a call

Ayesha- hello

Adriano- come to my cabin

Ayesha- ok sir

I went inside his office.

Adriano- bring my lunch and yours too

Ayesha- mine

Adriano- Hm from today onwards you are gonna have your lunch with me

Ayesha- but why sir

Adriano- i don't want to eat red chili again so that's why you're gonna eat with me

Ayesha nodded in embarrassment

After sometimes later~

I come inside and place the food on his desk and mine too

He looked at me and order to have it first i nodded and have mine 1st and after sometimes later he also start eating but no one dare to ulter a word.

After lunch i was about to clean the desk but adriano stop me by saying

Adriano- No need to do this.

Ayesha- but sir

Adriano- i say no need

He said in his dominating aura so i quickly say yes.

I was looking down but i grader my all courage and said

Ayesha- sir I'm very sorry for yesterday i don't know why i did that I'm sorry sir

I said looking down waiting for his reply but i didn't get any. I look up to see him but he handed me files

I looked at him being all confused

Adriano- do this before leaving

Ayesha- oh ok

I walk out from there. Annoyance is clearly visible on my face. He is really a jerk i was feeling sad for doing that to him but he clearly deserve that.

I said sorry to him at least he can nodded but no he decided to be cold ass jerk ughhh why did i even get this job. There are so many companies but no i have to get this job only. Now he also give me this work. How can i complete this files before leaving this is too much now. I can't bear this i can't even ask for help. Why he is so crual did i even did any bad thing to him. No Right so what is his problem. Why he always find me ughh he is really annoying

Let's do these files now. I don't want to stay here at night.

I start doing my work but it's too much i don't think i can complete this and it's also getting late. Everyone started leaving.

Some time later~

It's 10 o'clock now and I'm almost done. No one is here I'm all alone. I quickly do all my work and start to leave but suddenly some-one call my name from behind.

Ghosts there is ghost ooh nooo. I don't wanna die

Ayesha- no no please ghost uncle please i don't wanna die

I said without looking back being all scared.

Suddenly i feel someone touch my shoulder and i started to cry

Ayesha- pl_ease i don't wa_nna die I'm to youn_g too die no_w plea_se ghost un_cle

- shhh it's me

Chapter Six

Part~6

My tears started to flow. Now ghosts started to talk. I don't want to die so soon.

I turn back to see the ghost but found Mr Romano standing there. I run to him and hug him tightly.

Ayesha- S_ir th_ere is a gho_st

I was crying nonstop and i feel Mr Romano hug me back, he is trying to calm me down.

Adriano- shh there is no one is just me

I look at him then suddenly reality hit me, i was hugging him like there is no tomorrow, i break the hug and look at him confusingly

Ayesha- what ?

Adriano- there is no ghost, it was me

He said that and started to walk and i also follow him like a lost puppy

Adriano- you should have gone home it's too late now

Ayesha- sir you told me done the files before leaving

Adriano nodded

I came out of the cofice and started looking for a cab, then a car stop infront of me

Adriano- come in

Ayesha- sir it's ok i can manage

Adriano- i already saw how well you manage, come in i will drop you

Ayesha- ok sir

I walk towards the car and sit inside and give Mr romano my address, the whole ride was silent until my stomach started to growling, i look down in embarrassment.

Mr romano didn't say anything and stop the car near a small cafe , i look at him being all confused.

Adriano- come out and have something

Ayesha- but sir

Adriano- it's an order miss ayesha

I didn't say anything and started to follow him inside the cafe.

We both take a sit and i was just looking at him, did he just taking care of me or what ? Why he care if I'm hungry or not.

My thoughts got interrupt when Mr romano call me

Adriano- Miss ayesha, what you like to have ?

Ayesha- Risotto I'm craving for it

I told him without thinking twice

Mr romano order my dish.

After some time later it arrive

Ayesha- sir you didn't order anything

Adriano- I'm not hungry

Ayesha- Sir you can taste mine

I offer him but he refused to eat what a jerk, I continue to eat mine food it was really good. Mr romano just sitting there waiting for me.

After eating Mr Romano pay the bill , i told him no to but he just shut me up with his dominating eyes. So i didn't say anything. After that we again went inside the car and drove off

Mr romano drop me to my apartment. I just thanks him and went inside my apartment.

I'm was tired so i just slept.

Next day~

I was doing my work but again i got a call from Mr romano. He call me to his cabin

Ayesha- yes sir

Adriano- Bring me a coffee

Ayesha- ok sir

I didn't argue with him because he already told me that for someday I'm his secretary. So i just went to canteen to grab his coffee.

I was waiting for his coffee but then sam come towards me

Sam- hi ayesha

Ayesha- hey sam

Sam- seems like you're really busy those days

Ayesha- yes actually

Sam- if you're free then what about having lunch together

Ayesha- i really want but sam I'm having my lunch with Mr romano these day as I'm working as his secretary

Sam- what his secretary

Ayesha- yes actually his secretary is taking off for some days so

Sam- ohh but having lunch together it's...

I didn't let him finished his words and told him what i did to his lunch that day.

Sam is laughing like a mad person

Sam- ooh god ayesha i can't believe you did that oo god that's why he is having his lunch with you

Ayesha- yes that's the actual reason and please ha don't tell anyone about it. I only told you

Sam- don't worry i won't tell anyone.

Ayesha- oo my coffee is here. See you later bye

Sam- bye

I walk inside Mr romano cabin and place the coffee to his desk.

After sometime later~

I was working on my desk and Mr romano come and started checking everyone's work. He is shouting at everyone. Such a jerk.

Chapter Seven

Part~7

1 Week later~

Our project is finally done. Everyone work really hard this time. Mr romano help everyone . This week i saw a different side of Mr romano. I thought he cares for me but i was wrong despite of having a cold nature he really care for his employees and i liked that very much. This whole week i was really close with Mr romano. He helped me a lot. Maybe i start having feelings for him but I'm not sure about my feelings. I'm scared of getting rejected. I don't know what Mr romano feel about me. Sometimes he make me feel so special but i don't want to rise my hope because at the end it will hurt me very much. He is CEO of our company and having feelings for your boss it's not good. What will people think about me if they got to know. I'm scared. Scared of loosing him, scared of getting hurt.

Today is Sunday and i called my friends for lunch because i couldn't meet them due to work so i decide to invite them for lunch and i have so much things to share with them.

Jessica- So finally you have some times for us

Jessica come running and hug me

Lorenzo- I'm also here girls

Ayesha- i miss you so much guys

Lorenzo- yes we know that's why you done even have some time for us

Ayesha- no it's not like that. You know right i was selected for the project that's why i was really busy. I'm sorry

Jessica- yeah yeah we know. We are just teasing you.

Lorenzo- I'm really hungry give me food

Ayesha- i made indian food for you two.

Jessica- really *excited*

Ayesha- yeah let's eat

I serve them and they started to eat. They really like Indian food so i decided to make them some.

After lunch~

Jessica- Now tell me did you find someone

Ayesha- no I'm still finding my mafia

Lorenzo- ughh this girl

Jessica- fuck that mafia thing and tell me don't you like anyone ?

Ayesha- umm actually i like someone

Lorenzo- really tell me who is that unlucky person

Ayesha- what did you say

*I start hitting lorenzo playfully *

Jessica- now tell us about him .

Ayesha- he is none other than my cold boss

Lorenzo- what you fall in love with your boss ?

Jessica- office romance ooohhhhhooooo

Ayesha- guys stop it. I don't know what he feel about me. I'm scared it might be one sided

Jessica- tell us how did you fall for him

Ayesha- at first i didn't like him at all . He was such a jerk, cold, ass. And he always make me work too much. I hate him at start

Lorenzo- then how you fall for him ?

Ayesha- I don't know either.

Jessica- this girl ughh he might be handsome right ?

Ayesha- yes he is really handsome, you know what i did with him ? His secretary was absent for some day so he made me do his secretary work and one day he order me to bring his lunch to his cabin and i got mad so i mix red chili to his soup

Jessica and lorenzo started to laugh

Lorenzo- you mix red chili to your boss food. Thank god he didn't kill you.

Jessica- girl you have some guts

Ayesha- i know but he scold me for that

Jessica- did you thought he will give you chocolate for that

• They again started to laugh*

Ayesha- i did that because i was angry at him and i thought he will fire me from work but he didn't but guys one day after work he drop me at my place but before that my stomach started to make sounds because i was hungry so he stop his car at a cafe, i told him not to but he didn't listed to me and ask me to order anything but he didn't eat anything, he was just waiting for me to finish my food. He is such a boyfriend material. After that he drop me to my place.

I smile at them trying to hide my blusing

Jessica- someone's checks turn red due to blushing

Lorenzo- oooh god so romantic. I think he also like you but he don't how to say it. Men do that's things only for their woman and he is a CEO why would he stop his car and wait for you to finish your food. He like you that's why he care for you girl.

Jessica- that's how you fall for him. Why i don't have a love story like you

Fake crying

Ayesha- no actually i fall for him because i thought he only treat me like that but last week i realize he treats everyone goodly. He is cold but he has a soft heart. He just try to be a jerk but deep inside he is a sweetheart.

Jessica- if he treat everyone equally that's means you're not special to him. He treat you like he treat other employees

Ayesha- i know that's why I'm scared of getting hurt. And I'm Just a normal employee and he is billionaire . He would never fall for me.

Lorenzo- don't think so much negatively, be positive girls. I'm sure he also like you that's why he care for you.

Ayesha- he care for everyone

Lorenzo- but only shows to you.

Jessica- he is right but do you have his picture i want to see the person who stole my bestie heart.

Ayesha- hehe i have

• I open my phone and show them his picture*

See he is handsome right. He is my ideal type.

Jessica and lorenzo both are looking nervous while seeing the picture.

Ayesha- what happen guys why are you looking at him like that tell me. I'm getting nervous do you guys know him or what tell me

Jessica and lorenzo looking at each other, not knowing what to say

Jessica- Umm ayesha this is your boss

Ayesha- yes why are you asking like that ? what happen ?

They both look nervous

Lorenzo- um do you remember one day we went to a club

Ayesha- yes i remember

Lorenzo- and we give you a dare to sit on a strange lap

Ayesha nodded

Lorenzo- that day you were drunk ? Do you remember anything

Ayesha- yes little i sit on someone lap for some second and run from there.

Lorenzo- do you remember that person

Ayesha- No i didn't saw his face but why are you asking me? Wait don't tell me that..

Jessica- yes ayesha your boss is the person. Whom lap you sit that day.

Chapter Eight

Part~13

The next day~

Ayesha pov- i was doing my work but my mind was filled with The thought of Mr romano. Did he really remember that club night ? Does he knows that girl was me who sit on his lap ? Why did he select me for the project ? I guess my love was meant to be incomplete ! I should accept this before i started growing more feelings for him. If Mr romano still remember that night then i should apologize to him for my misbehaving nature.

Adriano pov- i was sitting on my cabin checking the profit of the new project. It's been 1 week. And everyone worked really hard and that's why this project is successful. Ayesha also improve her skill so much, she is quick learner, she worked really hard this week.

Ayesha pov- I'm done working on the files and went towards Mr romano cabin.

I knock on the door and went inside

Ayesha- sir I'm done with these files

Adriano nodded.

Ayesha was still standing, she look nervous. She want to say something but words are not coming out from her mouth.

Adriano- What happen miss ayesha ?

Ayesha- ye_s i mean_s no si_r

She look down bitting her lips

Adriano- you want to say something ?

Ayesha- Sir actually that day in club the girl sit on your lap she don't know that you're her boss and she say sorry

Ayesha was saying whatever coming to her mouth she don't know that she is saying due to nervousness

Adriano- club , lap what are you saying miss ayesha ?

Ayesha- i heard that an employee sit on your lap in club but but she don't want that you're her boss

Mentally slap herself for lieing to his face

Adriano- i don't remember anything like that miss ayesha. But why are you saying sorry ?

Ayesha- i don't know sir

Ayesha pov- maybe he don't remember anything ugghh How can you so stupid ayesha. So many people come to club how can he remember you.

Adriano- miss ayesha

Ayesha- ye_s sir

Adriano- where you lost ? I was calling your Name continuously

Ayesha- Sorry sir

Adriano- Hmm take his file and complete then

Ayesha- ok sir

I went towards his desk to grab the files and Mr romano Pull me by my waist and made me sit on his lap

I was completely shock my his actions for a minute i was blankly sitting on his lap and suddenly reality hit me and i try to stand but she tightly grab my waist not wanting to leave me

Ayesha- si_r w_hat ar_e yo_u doin_g

I said while stuttering

Adriano- that day you sit like this.... DO YOU REMEMBER

* I heart is beating fast. He remembers everything*

Adriano- i remember everything miss ayesha but you don't remember that

Ayesha- I'm sorry sir please forgive me. My friends give me a dare so that why..

Adriano- Shhh i know everything ayesha, you don't have to clearify yourself.

Ayesha again try to stand but Adriano pull her even more closer to himself

Adriano- why are you trying to run tulip

He call ayesha tulip as he know ayesha love tulip

Seeing ayesha nervous he finally let her go

Adriano- Tulip you like your nick name

Ayesha- sir yes mm no mm yes

He chuckle seeing her cute face

Ayesha didn't say anything and grab the files quickly and run

Adriano pov- so finally she remembers me now it's time to show her my love. I was waiting for this day to find this by herself.

I know that she got dare to sit on a strange lap and she choose me, she choose her fate. I fall for her when i saw her but now i fall harder after getting her know. She is an angel. She decided to say sorry it's shows that how Innocent she is.I can't wait to claim her mine.

Chapter Nine

Part~14

Ayesha pov- I can't believe what just happened, am i dreaming, did he really pull in to his lap. My heart can't handle this anymore.

I went back to my desk and started doing my work but my whole mind was remembering the incident happen few moment ago. I don't realized that someone is calling my name

Sam- ayesha , AYESHA

| I got flinch badly due to a sudden voice |

Ayesha- o_oh sam, you scared me

Sam- where were you lost. I was calling you from 5 minutes

Ayesha- ooh I'm really sorry

Sam- hmm it's ok ,

Ayesha- you want to say something sam

Sam- yes , are you free tonight ?

Ayesha- Mm yes, why did you ask ?

Sam- so can we have dinner together ?

Ayesha- why not

Sam- ok then i will sent you the location and time

Ayesha- ok

|| Ayesha got excited because it's been so long she didn't go out and sam is a good friend of her so she didn't find any reason to denied his invitation ||

She is smiling while doing her work but little did she don't know someone is watching her all moves

At lunch time ~

Ayesha pov- i just walking towards the canteen to have my lunch but suddenly someone pull me inside a dark room while covering my mouth, i didn't show his face.

That person remove his hand from my mouth, i was about to shut but then

- Sshhhh it's me

I was shocked hearing the voice because now i know who is this person

Ayesha- s_ir wha_t are you doin_g (shuttering)

Adriano- What did i do ? I didn't do anything till now

| Adriano pull ayesha more closer to him |

Adriano put his Head on her shoulder , Ayesha was so shocked to speak to his sudden move

Adriano- I love your smell, it help me to reduce my stress Amore

Ayesha- s_ir

Adriano- it's adriano for you amore

Ayesha was so confused by his actions in the morning and now she is even more confused.

Adriano- I want to keep you like this forever

Ayesha- b_ut sir w_e ca_n't h_ug like thi_s eve_ry ti_me

Adriano chuckled listening her words

He droke the hug and kiss her forehead

Ayesha was so shock to speak. word's are not coming out from her mouth

Adriano noticed her nervousness and said

Adriano- No need to over think so much , give some rest to your little brain

Ayesha- ye_s

| She don't know why she is nodded to him |

Adriano- tell me one more think, what sam was telling you ?

Ayesha- he...h_e invit_e me on din_ner

|| His eyes darken making ayesha scared ||

Adriano- why are you stuttering so much amore no need to fear me ok

ayesha nodded

Adriano- so you say yes to him

Ayesha again nodded

Adriano- so where are you going for dinner

Ayesha- he didn't told me anything yet he said he will inform me later

Adriano- this is for the last time you're going somewhere without my permission , next time if someone ask you out 1st you need permission and When sam inform you about the place you are gonna tell me with in a second. Did you understand amore ?

|| Adriano said being dominating and ayesha nodded multiple time seeing him like this ||

Ayesha- m_ay i go s_ir

Adriano- what if i say no

|| Now Ayesha whole mind is stop working ||

Adriano smile seeing her this nervous, he again pull her into a hug

Adriano- i can't see you with someone else amore. I hope you understand

Ayesha- Mm

Adriano started sniffing his head on her neck giving sensation to her whole body, he started giving her open mouth kisses on her neck. Ayesha want to stop him but her body is not with her mind. Soon Ayesha put her hand to his head pulling him more closer to her neck, giving him more space on her neck. Adriano smirk seeing his effect on her. he started kissing and sucking her neck leaving purple marks on there , ayesha started to moaning , hearing her moan adriano pull her more closer leaving no space between them, his hand started to crushing her breast softly and his lips started to kissed ayesha passionately ayesha also started to kissed him back, she can feel adriano smiling between the kissed, adriano started to suck her lower lips and grab her breast harshly. Ayesha flinch in pain and she came back to her sense she push adriano and run from the room without saying anything

Adriano pov- ayesha push me and run from there leaving me alone, i touch my lips and smile

Her lips taste good, I'm already getting addicted to her. But my intention was not kissed her so soon but i couldn't control myself seeing her this closer to me. Ughh she already had this much effect on me.

Ayesha pov- I don't know what happened to me, why did i allow him to kiss me or why i kissed him back but all i know i felt something different whenever he is with me. I always felt butterfly on my stomach.

I came inside the washroom and started to breathe heavily , my whole forehead is covered with sweat. Soon i turn towards the mirror and my whole world stop for a second. My whole neck is filled with hickeys.

What the heck. I touch there now i don't know how will i go out like this.

I started to tear up never in my life i kissed someone but now I'm facing this.

I take out my phone and call adriano because he is the one who cause this to me now he have to help me.

Ayesha- come to the washroom now

| I shouted because I'm getting mad |

Adriano- i was walking towards my cabin then i got a call from ayesha. Before i could say anything she told me to come to the washroom and cut the call. I got confused and went towards the washroom

Now I'm standing outside the washroom. I can't go inside it's female washroom so i call her and said to come out she told me that she can't came out.

I was tense why did she call me here without thinking twice i walk inside the washroom. Her back is facing me. I didn't see her face

Adriano- Amore

Ayesha move back towards me and my eyes fall on her neck. I smirked seeing my work on her neck. I'm feeling so proud, now no one can ever think to have her

Ayesha- Why you did this to me

| Ayesha was crying, her eyes are puffy due to crying and her nose already turn to red seeing her like this adriano hug her immediately |

Adriano- Shhh it's ok

Ayesha- no it's not

| Ayesha try to break the hug but adriano didn't let that happen and try to calm her down |

Ayesha- how will i go out, everyone will see me like this

Adriano- shh I'm here no one gonna see you like this ok

Ayesha is still crying , adriano cup her cheeks and look into her eyes

Adriano- why are you crying amore ? I can't see you like this, my heart felt heavy seeing you crying. I want to give you happiness, trust me amore.

Listening to adriano words ayesha stop crying. Soon adriano order someone to bring clothes.

Adriano- take this and change your clothes to this

Ayesha nodded and take the bag from his hand. Adriano walk out from the washroom and stay outside waiting for her

Ayesha Change her clothes into a turtleneck sweater that cover her neck fully

Soon she came out from the washroom

Ayesha- thank you sir

Adriano- it's ok amore , did you eat something

Ayesha nodded as no, she don't have courage to look into his eyes after he confessed his feelings

Adriano- let's go and eat something

Ayesha- but canteen time is off now

Adriano- don't worry i will order something. Come to my cabin

Ayesha- no no it's fine i will eat something later

Adriano didn't say anything because he knows she is not feeling comfortable now so he just simply nodded

Ayesha also back to her desk but got confused seeing sam there waiting for her

Sam- where are you ayesha

Ayesha- Mm actually..

Sam- what happen to your clothes

Ayesha- actually i split coffee so..

Sam- ooh ok actually i want to say that I'm sorry ayesha

Ayesha- why what happen ?

Sam- our manager just gave me alot of file and tell me to complete them today so i don't think i will have time for dinner. I'm extremely sorry

Ayesha- No it's ok it's fine

Sam nodded and went back to his desk

Little did now ayesha Know why manager gave sam sudden work.

Chapter Ten

Chapter~15

Adriano pov- Did that sam really thought i will let my princess go on a date with him. I can't allow anyone to look at her, she is mine. I will keep her always.

The whole day went like that everyone started to go and ayesha also started to pack her stuff but she is still thinking about that incident.

Ayesha pov- i came out from office and start waiting for cab but A car stop in front of me making me gulp it's no other then Mr adriano

He slow down his window. Asking me to sit. I don't have any other choice so i quietly sit and he drove his car. No one is speaking making the environment uncomfortableBut soon the car stop in front of my apartment. I didn't realize we are here. I thanks him and started to walk.

Adriano- Ayesha

Ayesha- ye_s sir

Adriano- I want to stay with you // He said straightforwardly //

Ayesha- what

Adriano- Yes

Ayesha- but sir

Adriano- tell me you don't like me

Ayesha- mm sir it's not like that

Adriano- Do you like me ? YES OR NO

Ayesha- yes

Adriano smile brightly, ayesha let him inside her house.

Ayesha pov- i let him inside my apartment and give him a glass of water to drink. I was just stearing at him without blinking. He look so tired but hot at the same time, he remove his coat. He is still wearing a white shirt but i can see his abs completely. I couldn't stop myself more and directly went and sit on his lap. Without giving him a Chance to speak i started to kiss him roughly soon he also start to kiss me back. The kiss is getting intense, soon he lift me and made me sleep on the couch. He started kissing my neck but due to my turtleneck sweater he is facing difficult. But i don't want him to stop today so i lift my sweater making him widen his eyes. Now I'm only wearing bra and jean. I take him towards my bedroom and started to kissing him. He started to kiss my neck again giving me pleasure. He push me onto the bed and started removing his shirt. Now he is half naked i started to touch his abs

Adriano- you like them

Ayesha- yes

Adriano- it's all your amore

He said that i smile and started to kiss his abs giving him pleasure he started to moan my name which made me more horny soon he made me sleep and hover me again started to suck my neck leaving purple marks on my skin. I was a moaning mess under him. I push him more towards me wanting more from him, he started to kissing my breast making me gulp. He is leaving a new sensation to my body. Soon he remove my bra making my breast visible to him. He is looking at my breast while licking his lower lips. In slip of seconds he started to suck my nipple, and his another hand was caressing my another breast. I was feeling so much pleasure he look me seeing me into pleasure he again started to suck my breast.

Adriano pov- I removed her bra leaving her half naked. My eyes got wided seeing her beautiful breast. I can't resist myself soon i started to suck them and my another hand started squeeze and press them hearing moans from her mouth time to time.. i couldn't control myself after hearing her sweet moan's, i started kissing her lips

she arch her neck back and moan into the kiss feeling his bare body rubbing with her bare body.his hands cups her boobs which make ayesha broke the kiss and throw her head backside.breathey moan left from her mouth.he start to placing open mouth kisses on her boobs and sucked the flesh leaving red marks.

he squeezing them hard while sucking them.he took her left nipple inside his mouth and start to sucking while biting softly.

Ayesha fisting the bedsheet tightly.Ayesha- emmmh (low moan).

he roll his tongue around her nipple and sucked hardly while watching her pleasurable face.

his hand went down between her legs and start to caressing her(*) making her eyes wide open.she rub her legs together while his fingers rubbing her(*) up and down.he left her boobs and giving wet kisses on her belly.her body shiver with his touches, kisses.he pushed his middle finger inside of her.

Ayesha- ahhemh(low moan).

he add another one making her fisting the bedsheet more tightly.he is kissing, licking, biting her inner thighs.he withdraw his finger and replace them with his lips.her toes curls up having him between her legs while eating her out.

Ayesha: emmmhah.

after doing his tongue magic down there he again went up near her face.her forehead full of sweat breathing heavily with eyes closed. she open her eyes and look into his eyes. Adriano- so sweet (kiss her lips).

this is the first time he is talking sweetly with someone.

Adriano- my sweet little girl.only mine(whispers into her ear). he pull his body up with one hand with other one he rub his *Ok on her entrance.she chocked into the air when he pushed inside of her slowly. Adriano clenching his jaw due to her tightness. she cry out and try to push him.

she is pushing him putting her hands on his chest while crying.

Ayesha- you are giving me pain leave me (crying) pull it out please its hurting (sobbing).

Adriano- hold her hands and pinned above her head.

Adriano- shhhhh my virgin baby.so innocent.pain will fade away baby.

he start to moving and she start to cry more.she try to pull out her hands but adriano hold them more tightly.

Adriano- my sweet baby (low groan).good girl your are taking me very good emmh.

after sometime later she hurt cries turn into pleasurable cry. he dig his face in the crook of her neck.

she arch her neck back giving him more access to her neck he hungrily sucking her neck while thrusting down there deeply. he free her hands and hold her waist and start to fucking her more deeply and roughly.she unknowingly run her fingers inside his silky black hairs fisting into them softly.

Ayesha- a-ahh adri-ano (m*an).

Adriano- yes my amore moan my name.

he pulled her into a kiss while fucking her deeply.he hold her legs make them wrap around his waist.

Adriano- you are doing so good Amore emah(low groan).

room fills with their pleasurable sounds

Ayesha press her face aside on the pillow while clutching onto the pillow beside her head tightly.he sucked onto her cheek.

Adriano- look at me(deep tone).

Adriano breathing heavily while breathey moan coming out of her mouth. he thrust hardly making her suck into the air hardly.

Adriano- look at me amore

she slowly look at him found him already looking at her. pleasurable tears falling down from her eyes. he Couldn't control and pulled her into a passionate kiss. he whispers into the kiss.

Adriano- you are only mine Amore. no one can take you away from me not even you.

Adriano pull her into a hug. And they both drifted into sleep hugging each other.

Chapter Eleven

Chapter~16

Adriano pov- I woke up as sunlight hit my face, as i open my eyes i saw the most beautiful person i ever thought about. I remember about last night, how we made love. She is hugging me like a kaola. Her eyes nose lips everything is perfect. I kissed her forehead , cover her with blanket properly and went to washroom.

After taking a bath i went towards the kitchen to make breakfast for my princess. I started checking for vegetables she had and guess what, her whole kitchen is filled with junk food only cookies, chips and instant noodles.

Adriano- is she really Indian ? How can she lived without Rice ?

I open my phone and call one of my men to buy groceries within 20 min and delivered to her address.

Meanwhile Ayesha pov-

I woke up today little late due to tiredness as i open my eyes last night memories flashback to my mind. I checked the other side of the bed but there is no one. Maybe he left. A sudden feeling of guilt arises. Ayesha- what had i done last night oo my god. He must left me what i was even expecting.

I started to cry hugging my knees. What have happens it's already happened I can't do anything about it now. I will call him. Why did he left me alone like this ? Doesn't he love me ? But he said that he love me then why he is not here now.

Adriano pov- One of my worker already delivered the groceries i ask for and i made vegetable soup for her. I know she is tired due to last night that's why i didn't wake her up and i also order pain killer medicine for her as i know it's was her first time and it's must be hurting her but i felt happy when i got to know she was virgin and I'm her first and i will be the last one she ever gonna have sex with.

I smile, take the bowl of soup in my hand and went inside her room as i walk in i saw her crying. She is crying while hugging her knee's.

I directly went towards her, place the bowl on the table and hug her tightly.

Adriano- Amore, what happen ? why are you crying ?

Ayesha pov- i was crying but then someone hug me and it's was no other then adriano. He cup my face and wipe my tears away. I hug him more tightly

Adriano- what happen amore ? Is it hurtingAyesha- whe_re wer_e you ?

Adriano- i was in the kitchen, preparing breakfast for you

Ayesha hug adriano and said - i thought that you...

Adriano cut the and said- you thought i left you alone

Ayesha nodded silently

Adriano place a kiss on her forehead and said- I love you amore not to leave you but to love you more, never thought next time that i will leave you because now i can't breath without you. For me you're everything and i will never let you go.I love you amore

Ayesha- i love you too and I'm sorry

Adriano- no need to say sorry amore now go get fresh up and have you breakfastAyesha smile and Stan up from bed.

She saw adriano was glaring at her She got confused and look down at herself. She was naked and standing in front of him like that she directly grab the blanket and wrap it around her

Ayesha- wha_t are you look_ing at huhhh don't you h_ave sham_e

Adriano- it was you who stand up naked and i already saw it all last night no need to cover yourself amore

* He said with a smirk on his face and started to going towards her and ayesha taking step towards backwards*

Adriano- why are you going backwards amore

Ayesha- pervert

Adriano smile at her word and said- only for you

Suddenly he grab ayesha and for this suddenly movement blanket fall down making her all naked again this time she blush seeing there closeness.

Adriano made her sit on his lap, making her face towards him and kiss properly. He pushed himself into her, making her feel his hardness as she moaned into his mouth when he bit her lips and took a chance to slip in. He tilted his head to get the proper angle as he made it deeper and more passonating But soon, his intense kissing was making her short of breath. She tried to shove him, but he bit her bottom lip instead, making her moan as he sucked there to ease the pain.

He stop kissing her after a while as he sense she was having problems to breathe, she open her eyes as he stop kissing her and her eyes meet his eyes. He is just looking at her without blinking while smiling as she got shy, she hug him and try to hide inside his chest he smiled at her cute behavior.

Adriano- Amore go get fresh up or i will lose my control

She nodded and run towards the washroom

After a while she walk out of the washroom while wearing a light pink sleeveless dress

Adriano was talking to someone on his phone as soon as his eyes fall on her he cut the call and look at her with a smile

Adriano- you're looking pretty Amore

Ayesha- thank you

She said with a low voice.

Adriano- let's have breakfast

Ayesha nodded and walk towards him. She was having problem to walk which got notice by adriano

They both sit together and start having their breakfast, adriano was feeding her and she was eating like a obedient girl

Adriano- is it still hurting amore

• She said looking at her with concerned*

She look down and nodded slowly, adriano touch her chin with his finger telling her to look at him and he place kiss on her forehead and Give her painkiller and a glass of water

Adriano- eat this, pain will go away

She did as he said.

And adriano started caressing her stomach to give her relief from pain.

Chapter Twelve

Chapter~17

Adriano- Amore

Ayesha- Hmm

Adriano- do you regret last Night

Ayesha- No i don't, i felt Love which i never feel

Adriano- I'm glad that i can express my feelings for you, I'm not very cool type person amore, discipline is something i want and I'm very workaholic person. Sometimes i can't express how i feel, I may not be your type, i can't say cheesy line nor i can sing for you but believe me i can give you happiness which you deserve, i will made you feel loved till my last breath tell me amore can i be your man ?

"YES" tear left from ayesha eyes and she quickly hug adriano. She feel something she never felt before her whole life, she want to hold him , kiss him, hug him for rest of there life.

Adriano- I love you so much Amore

Ayesha- I love you more Mr angry Bird

Adriano chuckle, "So that's my nick name" adriano ask, "yes, i gave this name" ayesha reply him while hugging him. "Why so, you could have give me a cute Name" "but this is also cute name"

Adriano- ok ok i understand mam

Ayesha nodded

Adriano- i want to say something

Ayesha- what is it ?

Adriano- You're gonna move in with me to my place

Ayesha- but

Adriano- no but it's final you're gonna move in, i want no discussion

Adriano speak in his dominating tone. Making ayesha nodded her head

Adriano- go and pack your necessary needs

Ayesha pov- i walk out from here to my bedroom. I don't know why i feel he is controlling me but i can't refuse him, i want to say many things but nothing come to my mouth maybe because of his aura but still it's been 2nd day of our relationship and he want me to move in i don't know but i don't feel it's right. Things are getting quick between us.

I started to pack my stuff, adriano also help me in packing.

Adriano- let's go my driver already arrive

Ayesha nodded and went out from her apartment with luggage's

They seat in his car~

Adriano notice ayesha was bit sad and didn't say anything to him.

Adriano hold ayesha hand, making ayesha turn her head towards him with a questionable expression

Adriano- I know you have many questions in your Head but trust me amore i just want to keep you closer to me so no one can steal you from me.

Before ayesha could say anything adriano kiss me softly and within a second she also kissed him back.

Adriano- I will answer your all questions when we are gonna reach home ok

Adriano smile and ayesha also smile while nodding her head

Adriano- i can't see you sad amore

He pull her into a hug

The car stop in front of a big mansion~

Adriano and ayesha came out of the car and ayesha eyes widen seeing the mansion

Ayesha pov- "it's beautiful no it's beyond beautiful, i never see this much beautiful mansion in my life"

My thoughts got interupt by adriano

Adriano- Amore let's go

Ayesha- Umm it's so beautiful house no no i mean mansion

Adriano smile and said "now it's all yours"

Ayesha blush hard

Adriano order his men to get her luggage inside the mansion

Ayesha and adriano started going inside the mansion and ayesha eyes widen seeing the beauty, everything is perfect and so elegant.

But one more thing caught ayesha attention~ Bodyguard there are countless bodyguard in the whole mansion. But why he is a CEO, then what these many bodyguards are doing here ?

One middle age female came towards us welcoming Us

- welcome home master and mam

Adriano- Amore she is head maid, and her name is mia

Ayesha nodded and smile at her

Adriano- let's go you must be tired, take some rest

Ayesha nodded and adriano take her towards his room

But ayesha noticed one more thing that not a single one maid or bodyguard look at her. Their eyes were down not having courage to look up at us.... But why ?

Chapter Thirteen

Chapter~18

M e and adriano enter inside the his bedroom. His whole bedroom is more big then my whole apartment but Everything is so dark, Every single thing is perfectly place.

Adriano- Do you like it amore ?

Ayesha- yes it's really nice but why everything is so dark

Adriano- because i like dark but if you're feeling uncomfortable then i can change into whatever you like

Ayesha- No no it's ok it's really beautiful

Adriano- now it's all yours amore please tell me if something bother you

Ayesha- Umm ok i will

Adriano and i was talking but our conversation get interrupt by a phone call. Adriano received the call and i notice his facial expressions change within a second after awhile he cut the call and looked at me with a straight face

Adriano- amore i got urgent work so i have to go , you can take shower you will free refresh and i will tell maid bring you luggage and don't forgot to have your dinner ok. Don't wait for me i might get late, love you

Ayesha- i love you too

he peck my lips and walk out of the room

I walk towards the washroom to take shower, as soon as water fell on my body i got goosebumps, did i made a wrong decision ? I don't know much about him ! What about his family ? Where did he go at this hours ? Why so many bodyguard are here ? I have to asked him about all this.

After shower i walk towards the closest as maid already being my luggage. I ware a simple top with a denim shorts and walk out of the room.

As i step outside, i can feel eyes on me everyone is glaring at me. I look at them with confused face and smile at them they all down there heads i don't think so much so i just went towards the kitchen to have something as i was very hungry.

As soon as the head maid sees me, she towards me running

Head maid- ma'am do you need something

Ayesha- Mm I'm hungry actually

Head maid smile at me and said- give us 10 min ma'am everything is almost ready, please have a sit

I nodded. She was about to walk out and i stop her and said

Ayesha- please don't call me ma'am, you're like a aunt to me

As i said that she shook her head in disagree and said- sorry ma'am i can't call you by your name it's an order by master, we can't disobey him

Ayesha made an o face and the head maid went inside the kitchen to bring her dinner

After sometimes later~

I had my dinner and went inside the room, Right now it's 12 At night, adriano told me not to wait for him but i have so many questions so i decided to wait but now I'm feeling sleepy due to tiredness and soon i drafted into sleep.

Adriano pov- i got some important work so i had to leave my princess alone, after my work done i came inside my mansion everyone came running towards me to welcome me but i ignore them and ask the head maid

Adriano- did she eat her dinner ?

Head maid- yes master

I didn't say anything and walk towards my bedroom.

I slowly open the door just to find her sleeping. I walk towards her, she is sleeping like a baby. I smile looking at her cute face, She is mine all mine now i can breath peacefully. I kissed her forehead and went towards the washroom to take a shower.

After shower i quickly ware my clothes and sleep next to hugging her.

Chapter Fourteen

Chapter~19

Adriano pov- I wake up as sun hit my face. I was feeling heavy on my chest, i look down and saw the person sleeping peacefully, her face doesn't show any worries it was carefree while those beautiful eyes are closed,

he extended his hand and tucked those hair strands behind her ear which were coming in between his eyes and the view of her face. He scooped her in his veined arms and peaked her forehead.

Ayesha pov- i woke up as i feel someone kissing my whole face, i started to giggle and wrap my hands around him, he looked at me with love in his eyes and peck my lips.

Adriano- good morning amore

Ayesha- morning Mr ice

Adriano chuckle and said "Mr ice , is my new name" i nodded is agreement making him smile again.

Adriano- ok ok now go get fresh up and come downstairs for breakfast

Ayesha- Ok

I went towards washroom to get fresh up.

After freshing up i wear my office outfit and went downstairs to have my breakfast

Adriano pov- i went to guestroom and take a bath there. Today is the first day with my amore, i want everything to be perfect for her, i know she is a picky eater So i told my maids ayesha's favorite dishes.

Ayesha pov-

As i walk towards the kitchen i can see adriano sitting there waiting for me to come. I went towards him and hug him from behind, and kiss his neck

Adriano- Someone is being naughty

I laughed at his compliment, he hold my hands and turn me towards his face, he kissed my forehead

Adriano- Come let's have your breakfast

I nodded and seat on a chair, he smiled at me and seat besides me.

All the maids started to serve our breakfast I look at the dishes and then at him

Ayesha- Love

I called him, he looked at me and asked

Adriano- what happen amore ? Why are you not eating ? Did you not like the dishes ? Should i told them to make something different ?

I looked at him in disbelieve

Ayesha- No it's not like that but..

I pause and started counting the dishes

Ayesha- 23 dishes really love. Don't you think is too much for breakfast

Adriano- no it's not. It's all your favorite, You always Skip your breakfast or eat those junk food.

Ayesha- but it's too much, i will get fat if i eat so much

Adriano- eat whatever you like amore and i wouldn't mind if you get fat

I looked at him being done and started to eat my breakfast, i looked his again giving him expression that it's amazing. He chuckle looking at me and start to have his breakfast.

Soon we both done with our breakfast, we stand up ready to go but my eyes fall on the head maid she was standing at the corner. I turn towards her and asked "did you made these dishes" She nodded "Yes ma'am" i looked at her , my eyes got wided thinking she made all these dishes "it's was amazing, thank you for the food" i said with a smile on my face but i can see she is feeling scared , before i can asked her anything, adriano interupt me and said "You can go mia" she nodded and went way from the dinning area leaving me and adriano alone.

I look back at adriano, his eyes are darker due to anger_

Adriano- AMORE LET ME TELL YOU ONE THING CLEARLY YOU DON'T HAVE TO THANKS ANYONE. THEY WORK FOR US AND I PAID THEM FOR THAT. DON'T FORGET THAT. YOU'RE THE QUEEN AND QUEEN NEVER THANKS ANYONE SO BEHALF LIKE A QUEEN

Chapter Fifteen

Chapter~20

Ayesha- Adriano

She call him, her voice is law. She is feeling scared seeing him like this, he is acting different suddenly,

Adriano calm down a little seeing ayesha like this, he realized he shout at her for thanking a maid.

He grab his hair in frustration than again look at ayesha but this time with love, he walk towards her but she is still standing on her place with her Head down

Adriano pov- I put my finger at her chin, making her look at me. As my eyes meet her, her tear escape from her eyes, i wipes her tear with my thumb and hug her. She didn't hug me back but her tears fall on my shoulder making my shirt wet, my heart ache seeing her like this, see is very sensitive but my anger take control.

Adriano- I'm sorry amore please forgive me

Adriano broke the hug and look at her

Adriano- amore i.. I'm so_rry

Adriano- i don't want you to say thank you or sorry to anyone, you're my queen amore, i want you to rule this mansion, I'm sorry for shouting at you amore. I'm sorry

Tear started to fall from adriano eyes, his heart is acheing seeing her all quite, i never thought i will make my amore cry.

Ayesha wipe his eyes and kiss his lips

Ayesha- it's ok but don't do this again

Adriano- i promise i wouldn't, I'm sorry amore. Please don't leave me

Ayesha- i will never leave you

Adriano hug her kissing her forehead

After a while adriano and ayesha went for office.

I was feeling little anxious, adriano saw my nervous state and said "what happen amore" i looked at him and place my head on his shoulder "Should we keep our relationship private" he hold my hand and started to rub it "why so, you don't wanna call to be my girlfriend ?" I shook my head "no it's not like that" "than you don't have to worry about anything amore" I hm in response,

"Do you understand amore" he again asked me, "Yes, i understand" he kissed my forehead.

In office~

Adriano told me not to worry about anything but still my heart is beating very fast, i want to told him the real reason why I'm so nervous but i can't.

I came out from my thoughts as adriano hold my hand and started to walk inside the office, i try to remove my hand but he give me a stern look, he is back to his cold personally, Ughh i can't do anything just walking with him

I can feel eyes on us, i lower my head due to embarrassment. I again try to remove my hand but he stop at his place looking at me and than again at the employees

Adriano- Why you all are stearing at us, do i pay for looking at me

He said in his cold voice making everyone gulp in fear.

Ayesha thought- does he has split personality, he was so lovely in car and now he is being a cold ass jerk

After scolding everyone he again hold my hand and start walking towards lift.

Only he and me and no one else. As the door close. Adriano pin me to the wall in a split on second taking my breath away.

Ayesha- W_hat are yo_u doin_g

Adriano- loving my girlfriend

He didn't let me say anything and press his lips on mine, kissing me hungrily. He press his whole body on mine, I started to moaning making him more wild.

Before doing anything further the door open, i push him from me making a distance.

no one was outside making me chuckle, i look at him, he was laughing at me

Adriano- Why so scared amore ? Do you think i care if someone see us like this ? I would love if someone see us like this , they will know that you are mine only mine.

Ayesha- such a pervert

Adriano- Only for you amore.

He kiss my lips and hold my hand while walking towards his cabin.

Again everyone started to look at us. Adriano stop beside my desk. Kiss me for the last time before going inside his cabin.

Chapter~21

As i look at my colleagues they all are looking at me with widen eyes, i nervously smile at them and sit on place trying to ignore theirs stares.

I was doing some paper works But someone call me, i look up and found sam.

"What was that ayesha" he ask me being all confused, i nervously smile at him while looking down not knowing what to say. "You both are dating" i look up and nodded my head slowly "what" he shouted being all shocked "How ? When ? Why didn't you don't tell me" "It's all happen very quickly, i didn't got any chance to tell you" i try to convince him seeing his disappoint face.

"It's ok and congratulations, i never thought that Mr romano will fall in love with someone" he said making me chuckle. He walk away towards his desk and i again started to do paper works until i got a call from adriano

"Amore come to cabin" he said is almost soft tone "coming" i cut the call and went inside his cabin

"Sir" i said making him look at me "Don't call me sir when we are alone" he said coming closer to me.

"Why did you call me" "Because i was missing you" he said making me laugh "it just 1 hours and you already miss me" he nodded and hug me, i started patted his back

Adriano- why are you talking to that sam ?

He said breaking the hug

Ayesha- he ask me about us and i told him that we are dating

He smile and kiss my forehand

Ayesha- so you were keeping an eyes on me ?

Adriano- yes because i don't want anyone to stole my girlfriend

I give him a sharp look

Adriano- Ok ok i admitted i was jealous

Ayesha- why ?

Adriano- because you talk to him while smiling i don't like that, you are only allow to smile at me.

Ayesha- i never knew you had this baby side

I smile laughing hard, while he was just looking at me being annoyed

Ayesha- he is just my colleague, and you are my boyfriend. No need to feel jealous of him.

He nodded,

Ayesha- so now can i go back

Adriano- No

Before i could say anything, he hold my waist and started to kiss me.

Lunch time~

Ayesha pov- I'm feeling very awkward, everyone got to know my relationship with adriano, some of employee looking at me being all amazed, some of them were looking disgust on me. There is some article on our office website about our relationship. I Haven't read any of that, I'm scared to look.

I was going towards the canteen to have my lunch.

Employee 1- Have you heard about Mr romano relationship with an employee.

Employee 2- Yeah everyone knows that

Employee 3- I can believe Mr romano can also feel in love

Employee 2- And just with a mere employee

Employee 1- She must have seduce him

Employee 3- Or maybe she is just using him for money

Employee 2- i think she is a whore

Employee 1- such a slut, they can do anything for money

I was frozen at my place after hearing all these think about myself, this is that i was scared of, maybe everyone is thinking same about me.

Without wasting any more second i ran towards washroom, Tear started to flow from my eyes. I couldn't control myself from crying, being a girl it always affect me about how people think about me, about my character. It hurt to see how people think so law about me where they didn't even know me. I wash my face, i couldn't let adriano know about it, he will get worried seeing me crying.

I walk out from the washroom, Started walking through the corridor, everyone is so silent through it's lunch time. I look here and there everyone is having there lunch in silence. No one is looking at me awkwardly which confused me even more.

I went towards my desk, before i sit on my place my phone started to ring, ooh i forgot to take my phone with me, I grab my phone from my desk i see who is calling me and it was no other then adriano, without wasting a second i received the call "Hello, where were you i Was calling you so many time why were you not receiving my call do ypu know how much worried i was" he said in one sentence not even listing to me "Come to my cabin now" before i can say anything he cut the call, i sigh and went toward his cabin.

I went inside his cabin and he started to walk towards me.

He hug me like there is no tomorrow

Adriano- where were amore ? I was so scared ? Why were you not receiving my calls ? Do you know how much worried i was ?

Ayesha- relaxed nothing happen to me no need to worried. I was in washroom and my phone was on my desk that's why i can't receive your calls

Adriano- nothing happened to you

"He look at my eyes, making me glup with his intense stare"

I nodded slowly

Adriano- why are you lying amore

I break the eye contact "I'm not lying" i said looking down, he hold my chin gently making me looking at him

Adriano- than why your eyes are swollen and your nose is red

I didn't say anything because i know if i say anything more i might end up crying.

Adriano- amore if someone say something to you or if you heard someone saying something disrespectful to you than you can tell me everything without thinking twice, I promise to protect you and i will do that no matter if i had to fight against the whole world, I can let go everything but not you.

Tears started to flow again i couldn't control myself anymore and started to cry in his embrace.

Ayesha- how did you know that ?

Adriano- I saw you going towards canteen so i decide to give you a company but before i could call you from behind i heard what the hell those stupid employees were saying about you.

Before i can do anything you run from there i thought to run behind you and stop myself and went towards those stupid employees to teach them a lesson

"Watch what you said about my girlfriend or i will cut your Tongue if i heard her name from your shitty mouth again" i said looking at them furiously

"You 3 can pack your stuff and leave i don't need this kind of employees in my office who disrespect my girlfriend"

Employee 1- si_r sir please sorry please don't fire us sir

Employee 3- we will never do that again sir

Employee 2- Sir please forgive us please give us second chance please sir

They started to beg but i didn't change my statement i left from there

I just worried about you that's why i was calling you so many time. Negative thought were roaming around my head

Ayesha- you fired them, why did you do that ?

Adriano- why ? They were saying bad think about you ? You should be happy

Ayesha- No no don't do that, tell them to join again

Adriano- No

Ayesha- please please they don't have other job how will they managed to live

Adriano- it's not my responsibility

Ayesha- everyone deserve a second chance please i request you.

Adriano- you don't need to request.

He said and call his secretary

I smile at him when he said he gave them a second chance just because of me.

Adriano order some food for us because i didn't had my lunch, we both had our lunch together and after lunch i came back to my desk adriano didn't want me go from his office but i know if i stay there he will not focus on his work.

Again i started doing my works and than sam came towards me

Sam- Are you ok ?

Ayesha- Yes

Sam- i was worried about you

Ayesha- why

Sam- because i saw you crying

Ayesha- it's ok I'm all good

Sam- i like how Mr romano stood by your side, seems like he like you very much

After hearing his statement i started to blush

After talking for few minutes with sam i again started doing my work but got interupt again by those same employees who were saying bad think about my character, they were looking down guilt is visible on there faces

Employee 1- we are so sorry ma'am

Employee 2- please forgive us

Employee 3- We are feeling very ashamed

Employee 2- we say so mean think about you but you give us a second chance

Employee 1- thank you very much

Employee 3- please forgive us ma'am we are really sorry and thanks for giving us one last chance we will never do that again

I just nodded and smile at them.

I was done with my work and started to pack my things because office time is over

I walk toward adriano cabin to check if he is done with work or not

Ayesha- Love

I called him, he look at me forming a smile on his face.

Adriano- let's go

Ayesha- you are done

Adriano- No but i will do that at home

Ayesha- it's ok i can wait for you

Adriano- But i don't like you to wait for anything

Hearing his statement my check started getting red

Adriano peck my check and grab my hands while walking outside his cabin

Again everyone started to look towards us but this time everyone is smiling looking at us.

Chapter Seventeen

Chapter~8 to 12

C hapter 8 to 12 got deleted for some reason that's why I'm again posting it.

~~~~~~~~~~~~~~~~~~~~~~~~~~~~~~~~

Ayesha- what

My heart is beating first

Mr romano is that guys. Does he know about it. Does he taking revenge on me because i sit on his lap. I'm confused does he knows everything. Why he didn't say anything to me ??

Jessica- you ok ayesha ?

Ayesha- y_es

Ayesha- he is taking revenge because i sat on his lap

Lorenzo- what revenge

Ayesha- he always overwork me. Give me alot of work, make work on the same file again and again. and i remember i got the proposal for the project the next day after we went to club. Did he does everything on purpose ?

Lorenzo- don't think like that ayesha. You got the proposal that's not a bad think moreover it's help you to learn many things and it's an opportunity not a revenge.
~~~~~~~~~~~~~~~~~~~~~~~~~~~~~~~~

Jessica- and if he want to take revenge he would have fire you from his company but he didn't do anything like that. He overworked you but you learn many things so it's basically benefits you

Ayesha just nodded

After some times later jessica and lorenzo went to their respective house.

i laid on my bed thinking about Mr romano.

Ayesha pov- i think i should say sorry to him before it's gets too late. He probably know about it. Ughh what might he have thought about me, shit i messed up so badly this time. I will say sorry to him. And i have to stop my feelings if he doing all this just to take revenge then i will get hurt even more.

Flashback

| That night in club |

Adriano pov- i came to a club to discuss about some important topics, i was sitting at a club like a king, discussing about some work. Then suddenly i girl came and sit on my lab. ON MY LAB. She dare to sit on my lab. Who is this girl she have this much courage to sit on my lap. The whole underworld is afraid of me and this girl ughh.

I was about to say something. Anger is clearly visible on my face, I move my head to see her but Couldn't say anything to her. My mind stop working after looking At her, She is beautiful. I was about to ask her name but she run from there like a little kid. She didn't even look back.

I was just looking at her running figure. SHE IS BEAUTIFUL. She doesn't look like Italian, Her cheeks is fully red. Her eyes were shinning like a diamond. The smell of her hair making me weak. I Want Her, i need her. Maybe by accident she got my attention but now I'm her destiny.

I Order one of my man to get her all information.

After 20 minutes later her whole information is on my hand. I started looking.

Name- Ayesha Bora, Age- 22 , Nationality-Indian

She work on my company. And i never know that. Look destiny want us to meet. I smile looking at her pictures. And order my manager to add her on our new project group. He was confused at first because she is new employee but couldn't ask me any questions and add her to my new project. Now she will stay in front of my eyes.

I never believe in LOVE but after seeing her i understand Why everyone is so crazy for love.

The whole night i can't sleep. My whole mind was filled with her thoughts. I never thought i will be this crazy over a girl. I just want her next to me. She already made me crazy. MISS AYESHA SOON TO BE Mrs Romano.

The next day~

Adriano pov- For the 1st time in my life I'm this much excited just because I'm gonna meet her again. I know she don't know me because last night she didn't even looked at my face. I want to know her more.

The whole car ride i was thinking about meeting her but i can't show how much I'm excited i have to maintain my cold nature in front of her too. But she already made a soft place for herself in my heart.

In meeting room~

I walk inside the meeting room just to meet the special person. My eyes were searching for her. I want to see her.

I was looking for her and my eyes cought a little figure, our eyes meet for a bare moment and she look back being all nervous. That's she. She is ayesha. She is looking more beautiful then last night. Her pink lips her hair her eyes everything is so dam perfect.

I want to put her on my lab again but i can't do that right now but soon.

Everyone is scared of me but not she. She is looking excited. Just like I'm excited to meet her. I moved back my attention from her to everyone and started to announce the project. After sometimes later i ask everyone if anyone has any questions. I know no one has courage to say anything in front of me but then ayesha speak.

Ayesha- Sir

Everyone looking at her with wided eyes

Ayesha- mm actually it's my first time. If someone can help me in understanding the process than it will help me

Adriano- Don't worry. You can ask anyone. I'm sure everyone will help you

Ayesha noddes with a smile

She is definitely different I'm impressed by her personality now. She is beautiful as well as knows how to raise her voice.

After the meeting end. I saw her talking to a male employee, I'm not feeling good seeing her talking to someone else but i can't do anything right now. ThenI saw her going back to her floor and i order my manager to move her to my floor. I want her near me.

I saw her coming towards her new desh. She started to put all her belonging. I was going towards her but stop at my place when i saw the same employee who was talking with her before, start to talk with her again. I went directly to my cabin being all angry.

I want to fire him right now but it's not right i have to be professional.

After sometimes later i call her ~

She came inside my cabin being all nervous.

Ayesha- Sorry sir i didn't know that you call me

Adriano- Hmm take these files and complete them within an hour

Ayesha- all of these

Adriano- Yes

I takes the files from my desh And went out. I know I'm being strict and it's not because I'm jealous, i want her to learn everything. I want her to do her best so no one can question her.

I again started doing my work~

At lunch break-

Adriano pov- i went out to have my lunch but my eyes fell on her, everyone is going towards canteen but she is still doing her work. I want her to do best but that doesn't mean i will let her starve herself. Work is not important then her health.

I went towards her desk and said

" You should go and have you lunch"

She look up and stood at her place

Ayesha- ye_s sir i mean no sir.. aa i mean i have alot of work to cover sir. If i had...

Why she is stuttering so much but she look cute being all nervous

Mr Romano- Go and have it

I said it coldly and went from her desk.

I came inside my cabin and look at her, she is happily going towards canteen

I smile looking at her cute figure

"Only she can made me smile lke that" i said to myself

After lunch break~

Adriano- come to office now.

I call her again because i want to see her cute face

She came after sometimes later

Ayesha- Sir actually

Adriano- what ?

"I said maintaining my cold nature. I really don't want to saw her my this side but i don't have any other options"

She look down being all nervous i understand she is not done with her work

Adriano- Miss Ayesha you are not done with the work i give ?

Ayesha- No sir actually some files are left

Adriano- Hmm do them before leaving office

Ayesha- Yes sir i will

She went out from my cabin. I know I'm being a jerk now. No one can do this much work in a little time but i want to tease her that's why I'm giving her alot of work or you can say I'm giving her little punishment because she didn't recognize me

After something later

Ayesha come to my office

Ayesha- sir I'm done with the file

I nodded and she place the files in my desk

I looked at the time and it's quite late so i tell her to book a cab , she nodded and went out.

After she left i couldn't control my smile. I was smiling like a crazy. She made me feel nervous whenever she is with me.

But it's quite late. Today it's her first day and i made her do overtime. Ughh she might thinking that I'm a jerk. But all i want to spend some time with her.

The next day~

Adriano pov- I told a female employee to call ayesha because i was missing her and want to see her cute face in the morning

After sometimes later she came

Ayesha- May i come in sir

Adriano- come in

Ayesha- yes sir how may i help you

Adriano- bring me a cup of coffee

Ayesha- sorry

Adriano- i said bring me a cup of coffee

Ayesha-ooh ok

I just call her to see her beautiful face but i have to give her a work. So i told her to bring me a cup of coffee. I don't want to overworked her but i want her near me every time and end up making her overworked. She must be cursing me now *I laughed imagine her face*

After some minutes later she came inside my cabin holding a cup of coffee

Ayesha- Sir your coffee

Saying that she put the cup of my desk.

I was checking the files she was working yesterday and she made many little mistake, i already knew she will make mistakes because she is just learning now. I can't expect her to be perfect in work now but i have to make sure she don't make any mistakes like this again.

Adriano- You have done many mistakes Miss ayesha

Ayesha- sorry sir but what are you saying ?

Adriano- you have to do this files again

I know I'm being crual now but she have to do her work right. She need to learn many things.

I looked at her she is looking down, maybe i shouldn't have said like that but it's for her own good. I grab the cup and take a slip.

Adriano thought- is she planning to make me diabetes patient. Who put this much sugar on coffee. I placed the cup and ask her

Adriano- what is this

Ayesha- si_r co_ffee

Adriano- i know but who told you to put sugar

Ayesha- No one

Adriano- than why did you put sugar

Ayesha- but sir you didn't even told me to not put

She is really something. I never meet anyone who dare to speak so frankly with me. But i like her attitude

She is right because i didn't told her anything about sugar so she put according to her wish but I'm concerned if she eat this much sugar it's not good for her health.

Adriano- leave it and take this files and this time don't make any mistakes

Ayesha- ok sir

She takes the files and went out. I smile when she walk out. Only i know how badly i want to kiss her pink lips. It's very hard for me to control myself whenever she is near me.

I was going towards washroom but i saw the same guy with ayesha. They are seem like really close. This time i couldn't control my anger, how dare he got close with her. I directly went towards ayesha desk and said

Adriano- miss ayesha.

She flinch a little by my sudden voice, she stand up on her place and that guy also stand up

Ayesha- Ye_s sir

Adriano- care to explain why Mr sam is helping you rather than doing his work

Ayesha- sir ac_tually

Sam- Sir actually i insists to help her. She was having difficulty so i decided to help

Adriano- if you have any problems why don't you ask me miss ayesha. I'm your boss right

Ayesha- I'm sorry sir

Adriano- sam you do your work and next time i don't have to tell the same thing again

Sam- ok sir

Saying that i walk inside my cabin. I would have punch his face, but ayesha was there and i don't want to make her fear me more. I Don't wanna show my different side to her.She has a soft spot in my heart but now she is making me jealous.

I walk towards my desh and slammed the desk. My anger was at peak now. I don't feel good seeing her with someone else and the way she was smiling with him make me more angry. She never smile at me but smile at that guy why ? I don't care if you like him Miss ayesha , you were meant to be mine and i will make you mine by hook or by crook.

In meeting room~

Adriano~ From today onwards we are going to work on our project and i hope no one gonna make any mistakes.

I told everyone that i don't want any mistakes because this is very important project for our company.

Everyone nodded.

After the meeting end everyone start going outside and my eyes were stick on that one person. She was about to go out but i call her

Ayesha- Yes sir

Adriano- miss ayesha can you please bring my lunch

Ayesha- sir it's not my job it's your secretary job

Adriano- i know and she is absent for some day so i decided to make you my Temporary secretary.

Ayesha- ooh ok sir i will bring you lunch

She went out being frustrated and i laught at her cute behavior, she don't hesitate to say no. I'm liking her even more. She is innocent she don't even think before saying anything. She is just my type or i can say she is just the way i want her to be.

I myself send my secretary to vacation because i want ayesha to be my side. My secretary was shocked because i give him a vacations but agree directly because it's rare to get a opportunity like this.

After some time later~

Ayesha came smiling a little. I'm feeling something off about it because i was accepting her to be angry but now she look very calm and happy.

She come inside and put the plate on my desk, she give me a smile which i didn't accept to receive.

Ayesha- enjoy your food sir

I nodded and she went outside.

After she went out i directly look at the food and i took the spoon and taste the soup and guest what she did, she put extra chilli on my soup. And laugh out loud. She is so bold that she dare to put chilli on her boss lunch. Woww she is something i have to say.

That's the reason she was so happy. But she didn't expect me to know that or what. I'm confused now.

I call her to come inside my cabin

Ayesha- hello

Adriano- come to my cabin now

She came inside being nervous. I was controlling my smile. She is scared now. But she didn't thought before putting chilli but now she is scared.

Ayesha- sir

Adriano- Shut up

I shout at her. I don't want to but she need to learn a lesson, she can't put chilli to someone's food like this, I don't mind that because i like her but no one will accept her this behavior, so i have to scold her. She need learn how to behave with her seniors.

Adriano- why did you do that huh

Ayesha- i don't know sir

Adriano- are you kidding me

Ayesha- no sir yes sir. Please sir sorry sir i will not do that sir forgive me sir

She was saying whatever coming inside her mouth. I can feel she is nervous and scared so i didn't say anything farther hoping she learn her lesson.

Adriano- this is your Last warning

Ayesha nodded being all scared

Adriano- you can go now

She went out being all sacred.

The whole day went like that i want to see her but she is scared and sad so i don't wanna make her more sacred.

The next day~

Adriano pov- i came to office and found ayesha doing her work but today she look sad probably because i scold her yesterday, i went inside my cabin and start doing my work.

I was doing my work and didn't notice it's already lunch time so i decided to call ayesha.

Ayesha- hello

Adriano- come to my cabin

Ayesha- ok sir

She came inside my cabin , her head is low I'm sure she is feeling embarrassed now.

Adriano- bring my lunch and yours too

Ayesha- mine

Adriano- Hm from today onwards you are gonna have your lunch with me

Ayesha- but why sir

Adriano- i don't want to eat red chili again so that's why you're gonna eat with me

Ayesha nodded in embarrassment and went out to bring our food, chilli was just an excuse. I want to eat with her and now she can't deny to eat with me. I smile in victory.

After sometimes later~

She came inside and put the food in my desk

I look up to she her. She is sitting quietly waiting for me and told her to eat , i don't want her to starve herself. she started to eat after that i also started to eat with her. I was looking at her she look so quite and sad but i can't do anything or she will find out that i like her.

After lunch ayesha started to clean the desk i told her no need to do this, i don't want her to do all this cleaning work. It's not her work to do.

Adriano- No need to do this.

Ayesha- but sir

Adriano- i say no need

She insist to do but sometimes later she agreed.

She is looking down and suddenly said~

Ayesha- sir I'm very sorry for yesterday i don't know why i did that I'm sorry sir

I was expecting her to say sorry but i didn't say anything and handed her some file to do

Adriano- do this before leaving

Ayesha- oh ok

She expected that i will say it's ok but i didn't say anything. Annoyance is visible on her face, i smile at her cuteness.

It's already 11 o'clock so i decided to leave, as i came i saw ayesha going outside it means she was working since morning, i started walking towards her but she stop at her place and started saying

Ayesha- no no please ghost uncle please i don't wanna die

I want to laugh so badly she thought me as a ghost, ooh god how can she be so cute, i walk towards her and place my hand on her shoulder

Ayesha- pl_ease i don't wa_nna die I'm to youn_g too die no_w plea_se ghost un_cle

But she started to cry making me panic and quickly make her turn towards me and hug her to calm her.

Adriano- shhh it's me

She is still crying hugging me tightly. My heart started to beat so fast.

She slowly looked at my face, she look surprised

Ayesha- S_ir th_ere is a gho_st

I was still hugging her, trying to calm her down but she look scared, she is even stuttering

Adriano- shh there is no one is just me

After sometimes later she calm down and broke the hug. I don't want to let her go.

Ayesha- what ?

Adriano- there is no ghost, it was me

I said and started to walk.

Adriano- you should have gone home it's too late now

Ayesha- sir you told me done the files before leaving

I just nodded, i realize i give her alot of work but not realize that she is not fast like other employee that's why it take her much time then other.

I came and directly went towards my car and saw ayesha standing at the road looking for cab so i park my car in front of her

Adriano- come in

Ayesha- sir it's ok i can manage

Adriano- i already saw how well you manage, come in i will drop you

Ayesha- ok sir

It's already late and i can't risk her to go alone so i decided to drop her, she came and sit beside me. No girl sit besides me it's her who sit in my car and i like it. I like the way it's feel. She told her address (i already know) and i started to drive

The whole ride was silent but her stomach started to growling. She must be hungry, i didn't thought that she is working for so long and didn't eat anything.

I started to look for a place where she can have something soon after i saw a cafe and stop the car.

She looked at me being all confused

Adriano- come out and have something

Ayesha- but sir

Adriano- it's an order miss ayesha

She must be feeling embarrassed but i know she wouldn't eat anything at home because she look tired, she wouldn't make dinner this late and i can't send her home hungry

We both sit, she is looking here anf there, i don't know what she is thinking about me but i can't see her hungry

Adriano- Miss ayesha, what you like to have ?

Ayesha- Risotto I'm craving for it

I ordered her dish

After some time later it arrive

Ayesha- sir you didn't order anything

Adriano- I'm not hungry

Ayesha- Sir you can taste mine

I offer me her food but i refused , i want her to feed me but i know she wouldn't do that. I was just looking at her, she look tired yet so beautiful, she is just focusing on her food , she is enjoying her food and i was looking at her without blinking. I'm already full looking at her.

After eating i pay the bill , she told me no to but i just looked at her and she shut her mouth after that i drop her at her apartment. She thanks me and went inside her apartment

I came home but my whole brain is full of her thought. I was smiling thinking how she hug me.

Now a day i start smiling because of her. She is becoming my happiness which i thought didn't exist for me.

Next day~

I called ayesha to my cabin

Ayesha- yes sir

Adriano- Bring me a coffee

Ayesha- ok sir

She didn't say anything and went directly.

After sometime later she came inside my cabin and place the cup and went outside, i didn't say anything because i was little mad. Everyone is making mistake which i can't tolerate.

~ Flashback end~

Chapter Eighteen

Chapter~22

Unknown- Boss i got some important information from our trusted man, there is someone who is keeping his eyes on us. Maybe he knows your true identity

:- What the fuck you guys are doing then, i need his whole information

Unknown- Boss we tried but there is no information about him

:- How is this even possible

Unknown- Boss maybe he is from our rival gang.

:- I don't care about anything collect his information as soon as possible and find out what is he trying to do

Unknown- Ok boss

Ayesha pov- I take a warm shower, relieving my body. Then i Applying body lotion and ware a comfortable dress.

Coming out from washroom my eyes are searching for someone but there is no one in the room.

"Maybe he is downstairs" i thought and walk towards the door but before i open the door and walk outside someone came inside and it's non other than adriano

"Where are you going amore" he ask me while walking close to me "i was searching for you, where were you" he was just staring at my lips without saying anything, i notice his gaze but before i could have said anything he smashed his lips on mine.

his lips were moving against mine..which felt so right after a hectic day. Placing my upper lip in between his lips, he gave me slow smooches letting me taste his love, bit by bit as my whole body warmed up by his actions. I softly tugged onto his lower lip as they got locked with his, He tilted his head to the left side, his right palm helping my head to rest on it while he gently allows me to rest my cheek on it. Looking into my eyes, he tucks a strand of my hair strands behind my ear softly.

"So desperate so see me amore" i chuckle "i can see who is more desperate Mr boyfriend" He laughed at my answer "i really love this side of you" "i have many different side also wanna see" i said looking into his eyes "I would love to" he is smiling in a teasing way "No way you're so pervert" i step back from him because i know what may came later "but i didn't say anything, and you call me pervert" giving me a smirk "i know you very well" he just chuckle

Ayesha- I have many things to ask you

He sit on our bed and said "what is it amore"

Ayesha- why there are so many body guards

Adriano- it's for safety

Ayesha- what safety

Adrinao- You know I'm a CEO right and i had many rivals against our company, anyone can try to harm us so that they can get our position in the market that's why i appoint them.

Ayesha just nodded but little did she is not convinced

Ayesha- One more thing

Adriano- what is it ?

Ayesha- what about your parents

He is silent while looking down

Adriano- They both die in a car accident

I became froze on my spot, did i hurt him while asking about his parents.

Ayesha- I'm sorry about it

He just smile at me and went inside the washroom to fresh up

I was sitting on the bed waiting for him to come so we can have our dinner together.

After sometime later he came back while wrapping a towel around his waist.

Chapter Nineteen

Chapter~23

Adriano- Amore

Ayushi- Hmm

Adriano- Tomorrow we have to attend a party

Ayushi- What party

Adriano- Our success party, everyone work really hard so i decided to throw a party

Ayushi- That's great but you should have informed me before

Adriano- Why what happen ? If you say i will postpone..

Ayushi cut adriano and said " No no need to postpone the party it's just i have nothing to ware"

Adriano looking at her with widen eyes

Adriano- Amore you have 2 wardrobe filled with clothes and most of them you have Never tried for once.

Ayushi- That's the problem i never try so i don't know what to wear.

Adriano- It's ok..party is in the evening so we can go shopping in morning

Ayushi got excited and hug adriano.

They both sleep hugging each other.

Next morning~

Ayesha pov- Me and adriano get ready for shopping, i was really excited because this is my first time going shopping with him.

As we reach the shopping mall people started staring at us it's probably because everyone know adriano, but he seems unbother.

Adriano was holding my hands like i was about to run.

We ignore everyone and enter one of the most expensive shop, i refused to go there but adriano didn't listed to me.

Adriano- Amore choose whatever you like

Ayesha- Let's go to some other store

Adriano- Why don't you like this design

Ayesha- No it's all very beautiful but too much expensive let's go from here

I grab his hand and started to walk but he stayed at his place, he didn't moved a inch, he is just looking at me or you can say glaring at me

Adriano- You are my girlfriend ayesha, my soon to be wife do you think i give a shit about these prices, i can give you everything you asked for even if you say "you want a star" i will give you one.

"Pack everything" adriano said to the staff, hold my hands and walk out from there.

Ayesha- Adriano it's too much, i don't need so many clothes

Adriano- Nothing it's too much for you amore.. i want you to look beautiful, i want to show everyone that now "you belong to me" no one is even allowed to looked at you.

Ayesha- Adriano stop joking around like this, you are scaring me now

Adriano just smile at her and didn't say anything farther.

Evening~

Ayesha pov- I wear a backless cherry red dress and put little bit of makeup.

I was wearing my heels than i feel like someone is watching me, as i turned back i found adriano looking at me with desire in his eyes

Adriano- Amore, let's not go there, we can spend some time here.

He said while stepping closed to me, grabbing my waist making me close to him, he place a kiss on my lips looking at my eyes with full of love

Adriano- I thought i will make everyone know that now you are mine but now I'm jealous because everyone going to looked at what's mine.

Ayesha was about to say something but adriano stop her by kissing her neck, he started giving her open mouth kisses, sucking her neck leaving purple marks on there.

He smirked seeing his work on ayesha neck

Adriano- Now everyone will know that you are mine.

Chapter Twenty

Chapter~24

"L et's go" Adriano hold my hands.

We reach there, walking towards the entrance i saw many people, some of them are my colleague.

Everyone is looking at us making me nervous.

"You are looking breathtaking amore" adriano whisper in my ear, i chuckle while giving him a smile

Adriano was introducing me to his business partners when a man came and hug him

Adriano- Amore meet Enzo, my very close friend

Ayesha- Hello, myself ayesha

Enzo- hello ayesha, I'm enzo

Adriano- she is my girlfriend or you can say my soon to be wife

*Adriano said making ayesha blush"

They both talk for some times than enzo went towards some other people

Ayesha- is he also a business man ?

Adriano- No he is a mafia

Ayesha- what ? Mafia ? Really ?

Adriano- Hmm he is a real mafia, why are you scared ?

Ayesha- No No I'm excited

Adriano looked at me "excited for what"

Ayesha- because he is mafia and i like mafia, i always want to meet mafia

Adriano- you are the only girl who love mafia, everyone is scared of them

Ayesha- well I'm not scared of them, i like them

Adriano- they are not how you think, they are crual very crual

I was about to say something but adriano got a call.

"I'm coming in a minute amore, Don't go anywhere and don't sit on some strange lap" adriano said, i just close my eyes in embarrassment.

Unknown - Did you find out who is that person is ?

Unknown 1- No boss but I'm sure he is from our rival gang

Unknown- I want his information within 3 days, infrom our all hacker to get his real identity and what he is planning to do

Unknown- Ok boss

Ayesha pov- i was waiting for adriano, looking here and there

Sam- hey ayesha

Ayesha- oo hey sam

Sam- you are looking so gorgeous

Ayesha- thanks

Sam- why are you standing alone where is Mr romano

Ayesha- oo he went to attend a call

Sam- ohh by the way ayesha I'm feeling very bad

Ayesha- why what happen

Sam- i told you that i will take you for lunch but i can't

Ayehsa- it's totally ok sam we will go some other day, no worries about it

Sam- really, thank ayesha

After talking to sam for sometimes i came towards the bar area but before i asked for some drink adriano made an announcement

Adriano- Hello ladies and gentlemen, I'm very glad that you all came here to celebrate our company success and in this wonderful environment i want to announce something very important, i never thought that i will fall in love with someone, i never thought that someone can ever love someone like me but i was wrong, i fall in love with a very beautiful woman not only by face but also by heart, she fullfil my emptiness that i never know existed, she melt my cold heart and manage to get a soft spot, I Love Her and i will make her my queen, i will do anything she asked me to do, her head with only go down for her, so Miss Ayesha Can i be you husband for rest of your life, will you give me the happiness that i always dream about

Ayesha pov- Tear started to flow from my eyes, i can't express how happy I'm, i slowly nodded my head

Adriano run towards me and hug me, he kneel down while taking a ring from his pocket

Adriano- will you marry me amore

Ayesha- Yes i will

Adriano made me wore that ring.

I get my happy ending........

Or not........

Chapter Twenty-One

Chapter-25

Everyone is congratulating us, adriano is busy talking with some business man

I excuse myself and came to washroom. I was about to enter but someone hit my head and i blackout

Ayesha pov- I feel Sharp pain in my head, i try to touch my head but... But my hands are tied.. tied with a rope

I was terrified not knowing what happen to me, i try to shout for help but my mouth is ducttap

Slowly i get my sense back... Someone kidnap me. I was in a abandoned room

Adriano pov- I Couldn't find ayesha, she is no where. I checked every single room but i can't find her

Adriano- Find my ayesha or i will ki‖ You all here

Adriano say to his man

Adriano- it was so tight security how can someone break down my security

Enzo- Boss Someone is trying to hack our information

Adriano- Who tf has so much audacity to kidnap "The underworld mafia fiance" he doesn't know what Adriano can do

Enzo- Boss we track their location

Adriano- let's go.. if something happen to my princess that i will cut him in thousands of pieces

Meanwhile ayesha- i started to cry in fear, i don't know what just happened why someone kidnapped me

: OOh You woke up ?

A voice came from my behind but the voice is very similar...

The man came in front of me. Showing his face... It's.. it's Sam...

Chapter Twenty-Two

Chapter~26

I was confused, I don't know how to react.. did sam kidnap me

Sam remove the ducttap from my mouth

Ayesha- S-sam.. wh-at is this.. wh-at are yo-u doing

Sam chuckle and said "look Ayesha, i have no problem with you but you are the one who came into the problem.. my intentions was never hurt you but you are the only key which will help me"

Ayesha- wh_at do you mea_n

Sam- That MF didn't tell you anything right... I thought he was using you but you turn out to be his fiance

Ayesha- What you mean say clearly

Sam- So desperate to know about you Fucking boyfriend uff sorry fiance, he is not the one you think. He is a killer... A fucking killer, he killed my brother. And i will kill you in front of him.. he have to face how it's feel to loss your love one

Ayesha- Stop your nonsense sam.. i know adriano. He can never do that.. you must have a misunderstanding

Sam- ughh you know nothing about him right ? He is not the one you think ayesha... He is the king of underworld mafia.. he is a fucking mafia king..

Ayesha- No he is not a mafia

I shout at sam within a second i felt shape pain in my right cheeks

Sam slap me so hard that my lips started to bleed.. He grab my jaw harshly

Sam- DON'T YOU DARE TO RAISE YOUR VOICE AT ME OR I WILL KILL YOU RIGHT NOW

Ayesha- Sam..

Sam- You want proof wait i will show you video footages

Sam bring his phone in front of ayesha playing a video..

Ayesha couldn't watch the video as it was very brutal.. adriano was ki||ing people mercilessly

Ayesha couldn't understand what she will do now... She scared of sam and now she is even more scared of her fiance

She is feeling betral..

Sam- See your lovely fiance.. huhh you know what ayesha when i first saw you i like you but when i start noticing adriano behavior towards you i understand everything.. I got to know he like you and you also like him.. it's not your fault.. you just fall in love but with the wrong person..

Sam- i can give you a chance to live.. but you have to live with me.. i will claim you mine.. ki||ing you is not enough to suffer him.. i will make him regret everything..

Chapter-27

Ayesha- Never.. i will never do that.. Ki|| me if you can but don't think i will sacrifice myself for a monster like you

Sam got angry listening to ayesha. He grab her hair harshly

Sam- MONSTER.. YOU CALL ME FUCKING MONSTER.. .*Slap* I gave you a chance to stay alive but your dumbas$ refused it.. Ok than get ready to die

Sam put a pocket knife in Ayesha throat

But before sam can hurt ayesha.. someone push him away from ayesha.. and it's non other than Adriano

Adriano punch sam multiple time..

Adriano- you fucking peace of shit.. how dare you to Kidnap my ayesha

Adriano continuesly punching sam.. Sam mouth and nose started to bleed.

Enzo came running and untied ayesha.. ayesha was crying silently.. she don't know what to do.. she is traumatized

Adriano- I could have ki|led you with you brother but i did mistake leaving you alive

He said to sam..

Adriano order his man to take sam to his basement

Adriano saw ayesha.. who is crying.. her nose is red.. lips are bleeding.. also have a slap mark in her cheeks

Adriano- Ayesha

He try to hug Ayesha but she flinched hard.. adriano thought she is scared that's why she is behaving this way

He try to make her clam and they both went to their home

In adriano house

Adriano made sure ayesha take propose rest.. he called doctors to check up on her.. But ayesha is continuesly crying.. adriano try to feed her but every time he came closer to her she get scared

Adriano- princess please eat something.. you are very weak.. your body need protein. Please eat something princess

Ayesha- I.. i.. do-nt... Wann-a st-ay.. here

Adriano- You don't wanna stay here.. you want to go somewhere princess..tell me where you wanna go.. i will take you

Ayesha- i wa-nt break-up

Adriano- princess it's not time to say jokes

Ayesha- I'M NOT JOKING MR ADRIANO.. I DON'T WANNA STAY WITH YOU.. YOU'RE A MU*DERE*... YOU KI|| PEOPLE.. YOU ARE A MAFIA.. YOU LIED TO ME

Adriano understand sam told ayesha everything... And she is upset with him for lieing to her.. she has rights to get angry on him.

Adriano- Princess please first listed to me please

Ayesha- No i want breakup

Adriano- at least give me a chance to explain

Ayesha was silent but her tears are still coming from her eyes.. adriano wipe her tears and kissed her forehead.. he made her sit on a bed.. i kneel down in front of her

Adriano- First of all.. I'm sorry that i never told you about my real profession that's only because i thought you will get scared of me but when i got to know you like mafia, i decide to tell you everything but before i could do that's sam kidnapped you.

And about sam yes i ki||ed his brother.. you you remember when i told you about my parents.. i told you that they died in an accident, i lied to you.. they were not died in a accident, sam's brother ki|| my parents in front of me...

My dad was also a mafia king but i always used to stay away from hus mafia business but one day his rivals (Sam's brother) ki|| my parents for mafia position infront of my eyes

They leave me alive to die by my own but i didn't.. i want to take my parents revenge.. As i grow up i became stronger.. and again one day i take my dad's mafia possion from them..

Now tell me what will you do if someone do that to your parents ayesha.

Adriano started to cry.. ayesha quickly hug Adriano

Ayesha- I'm sorry please forgive me.. i never knew you go through this

Adriano- no I'm sorry i should have told you before.. I'm sorry

Ayesha- it's ok now..

Adriano- That's mean you forgive me

Ayesha nodded

"Thank you so much ayesha for giving me another chance and for stay with me"

I love youI love you too

The End